Pat Ingoldsby occupies a unique position in Ireland. Just when you have classified him as a children's entertainer he broadcasts the kind of poems that jam RTE's switchboards.

As a playwright, his works — *Hisself* and *When Am I Gettin' Me Clothes?* — have been performed at the Peacock Theatre while *The Case Against The Full Shilling* was staged at both the Gaiety and the Project Theatres.

His two fantasies for children — *Rhymin' Simon* and *Yeukface The Yeuk* were commissioned and staged at the National Theatre. *Rhymin' Simon* subsequently toured the 32 counties under the Abbey Theatre banner.

RTE Radio Drama have broadcast six of Pat's plays to date. ABC Australia transmitted *The Case Against The Full Shilling* in 1989.

Six collections of Pat's poems have been published to date. He regularly performs his work on radio and television. Pat has also written best selling books of zany tales for children which have also appeared on tape. His poetry readings in universities, art centres, pubs and theatres are as unpredictible as they are exciting.

He has worked on RTE Radio as a disc-jockey, made documentaries, vox-pops, hosted the *Saturday Live* T.V. chat show, written television drama for children, short stories and comedy series for radio, conceived and presented the hugely popular *Pat's Hat, Pat's Chat,* and *Pat's Pals* T.V. shows.

He loves rock music, soccer, Chinese food, cats and snooker. His ambition is to keep changing, to face new challenges even though they scare him, and to find peace in his head.

Also by Pat Ingoldsby

POETRY

You've Just Finished Readi~~ ~~~ ~~~
Rhyme Doesn't With Reason
Up The Leg Of Your Jacket
Salty Water
Scandal Sisters

FOR CHILDREN

Zany Tales
Tell Me A Story, Pat (cassette)

WELCOME TO MY HEAD

Lots of love
to YOU!

from

1/11/2002
CLONTARF

Welcome to my Head

PLEASE REMOVE YOUR BOOTS

ANNA LIVIA PRESS

First published in 1986 by
Rainbow Publications

ANNA
LIVIA

This edition, 1991, published by
Anna Livia Press,
21 Cross Avenue,
Dún Laoghaire,
County Dublin.

Copyright © Pat Ingoldsby, 1986, 1990
ISBN: I 871311 13 6

Cover by Bluett
Cover photograph by Colm Henry
Typesetting by Mick Ward
Printed in Ireland by Colour Books Ltd.

For Ruth, Brig, Willow,
Blackie and Hoot
with love and Tuna Whiskas

CONTENTS

BEFORE SHOCK TREATMENT

BOOT-BOY BUDGIES RULE!

Basil the Boot-Boy Budgie,
Was browned off in his cage,
So he put on the denims,
Got his Budgie-Bovver-Boots,
And went out on the rampage.
He threatened middle-aged Mynah Birds,
And booted pensioner parrots,
Then off to the rabbits' All-Nite Caff,
To sniff some cocaine carrots.
Clutching his trusty aerosol tin,
He had this message to spray,
"Bleedin' canaries rule all wrong,
But budgies rule . . . O.K.!"
While wrecking the parrots' pool-hall,
He noticed Denim Dinah,
Some budgie bootgirls is bleedin' fine tings,
But she was bleedin' finer!
Basil began to bill and coo,
She said: "Watch who you're bleedin' cooin'",
But Basil was a Bay-City Budgie,
He knew what he was doin'.
They settled down in a County Council Cage,
and abandoned their Boot-Budgie ways,
Every Sunday they're at first Mass,
And they've hung up their aerosol sprays.
Sometimes when the kids are asleep,
They kneel in silent prayer
"Bless our little Bay-City Budgies,
Don't let them go to the tear.
Keep them safe from bovver-boots,
And trousers at half mast,
We know we've been bad budgies,
But all that's in the past."

Then Basil sheds a gentle tear,
He doesn't know what to say,
When he sees what the kids
Have written on the wall,
"DADDY BLEEDIN' RULES . . . O.K.!!!"

I WANT TO BE ALONE

Walter Woodpecker won a Master's Degree,
After drilling his millionth hole in a tree.
His proud mother couldn't help shedding a tear
when her son was nominated "Woodpecker of the Year".
Next day came a thousand sacks of fan mail,
Plus an invitation to lecture at Harvard and Yale.
Proposals of marriage filled every post,
He gave them some thought as he buttered his toast.
Press and TV men appeared by the score,
While autograph hunters queued at his door.
At night he lay down his poor weary head,
Photographers pounced out from under the bed.
Walter was forced to creep out in disguise,
To personally accept the Nobel Pecker's Prize.
Society columnists linked Walter's name,
With Lady Sarah Sawdust of debutante fame.
"Lady Sawdust is merely a very good friend,"
Said the Woodpecker, whose patience was nearing its end.

That night while reporters and cameramen slept,
Off into the darkness the Woodpecker crept.
Some say he became a Carthusian monk,
Others say he hid up an elephant's trunk.
The best clue of all is that the Nth. and Sth. Poles,
Have just been mysteriously riddled with holes.

CAN YOU TELL?

It's no fun being an identical twin,
Ask Michael Pim and Michael Pim,
Michael is married while Mr. Pim is not,
The wife is still wondering which one she has got.
Michael's called Meehawl while Mick is called Mike,
Which simplifies matters as they're both so alike.
Meehawl is bald while Mike has no hair,
Which makes it so easy to identify the pair.
If you still can't distinguish one from the other,
Simply remember . . . Meehawl's Mike's brother.

A FOOTNOTE

It's agony trying to make ends meet,
When attempting to scratch your head with your feet.

SLIGHTLY NUTS

A neurotic young squirrel called Cynthia Fleeces,
Was convinced that her nerves were going to pieces,
She smoked at least fifty cigars every day,
And her twitchey tail began turning quite grey.
One night she ran thirty-five miles in her sleep,
And finished joint third in the Grand Irish Sweep.
She decided there was only one thing to do,
So she telephoned Professor 'Too-Wit, Too-Woo'.
There was nothing this wise old owl didn't know,
Like embroidery and Latin and what made rivers flow.
He had degrees in 'Too-Witting', not to mention
  'Too-Woo',
And lectured in the college that distilled Irish Stew.

He listened to Cynthia through a magnifying glass,
And made notes in sign-language on a piece of long grass.
Then the professor tried treatment by shock,
He swooped unexpectedly from a Grandfather clock.
The effect on young Cynthia was truly dramatic.
She fled to the safety of a 12th century attic.

Some say she's cured and others, she's not,
We think the squirrel is now smoking pot,
Because a sign on her door, with a pink paper clip,
Says: "Away for six months — Am taking a trip."

THE WAYWARD MICE

A teenage mouse called Mabel,
Placed her elbows on the table,
Grandad lamented about young mice,
Who had no manners around the hice.
Mabel wore a maxi-skirt down to her feet,
Which Grandma considered indiscreet,
Advising Mabel it's completely wrong,
To wear a garment two inches long.
"Just supposing a cat gives chase,
It's going to be a one-sided race."
Mabel laughed and powdered her nose,
"Old fashioned grannies — sure anything goes."

A twenty mouse called Nigel Hoots
Pulled on his pair of leather boots,
Combed his sideburns, donned his jeans,
And borrowed his sister's scarf for teens,
His brushed his moustache just like Clark Gable,
Only the best was good enough for Mabel.
"If you go out you blatant sinner,
Dressed up like a dog's dinner,
You know where you'll finish."
His mother cried.

And something tells me she meant,
A pussy's inside.

The lovers met in the dining room,
Embracing in the gathering gloom,
So passionate were the kissing mice,
They completely forgot their elder's advice.
"I love you Mabel" said Nigel Hoots,
Admiring his reflection in his boots.
"I adore you, Nigel" said Mabel fair,
As they snuggled under a Queen Anne chair.

A hippy pussy called Ponsonby Odd,
Took one look and said 'Mother O'God,
That LSD is mighty powerful stuff,
And me, I've taken more than enough,
I'm packing all this drug taking in."
And those shameless young mice,
They're living in sin.

FLAMING FELICITY

Felicity, the world's only fire-eating snake,
Was furious when people said her act was a fake.
To prove herself she swallowed a blazing garden shed,
And felt a glorious rush of central heating to her head.
She sprinkled salt and pepper on a fresh electric fire,
Which made a tasty sandwich with a dash of copper wire.
Her critics still weren't satisfied and shouted "We want
    more!"
Felicity tried her best to eat a fried revolving door.
But snakes have sensitive tummies, just like you and me,
The first time that she hiccupped, she scorched a hollow
    tree,
Poor Felicity's heartburn was the hottest ever known,
The doctor stood six miles away with an asbestos telephone

"Take two fire extinguishers daily" was what the doctor said,
"And a fire brigade with water, before you go to bed."
But Felicity had different plans and now you'll hardly know her,
She works a 42 hour week as a hiccupping flame-thrower.

DEEP IN DINGLEY WOOD

All hail to the rabbits of Dingley Wood,
Who behave themselves perfectly as good rabbits should.
They deny themselves carrots all during Lent,
And seldom get into arrears with the rent.
At church on Sundays you'll never find them late,
And they give tons of lettuce when they pass round the plate.
The only exception was a rabbit called Clore,
Who found being good was a bit of a bore.
He read naughty books and dated bunny girls,
And wore his hair long in a tangle of curls.
He roared round the forest on a 650 scooter,
And terrified old bunnies when he sounded his hooter.
Not only that, but he used awful words,
And told little bunnies about the bees and the birds.
"This scandalous behaviour has gone far enough,"
Said the Reverend Rabbit, as he passed round the snuff.
"It's got so old bunnies can't go out at night,"
Said a pensioner rabbit whose tail twitched with fright.
They all agreed that something had to be done,
Because life was impossible with this terrible 'bun'.
That midday at morning before evening began,
Let's just say — 'Someone suggested a plan',
Next day as he roared down the Willow Tree Trail,
I wonder what caused his disc brakes to fail,
I'm certain it was no one from Dingley Wood,
I mean — they ALWAYS behave as refined rabbits should.

GERTRUDE THE GREAT

Gertrude the Granny Grasshopper,
Was determined not to retire,
With a prodigious leap of fifty gallons,
She cleared a cathedral spire.

Her grandchildren pleaded with Gertrude,
To behave as old grasshoppers should,
To write her memoirs and drink warm milk,
And get a pension book if she could.

But Granny Gertrude had other plans,
And nearly destroyed us all,
When she started a world-wide red alert,
By hopping the Berlin Wall.
Now she was completely out of control,
And caused diplomatic complication,
As clad in woolly pink bedsocks,
She sprang from nation to nation.

The Soviet leaders made a speech,
Calling Granny 'A Capitalist Plot',
The U.N. held an emergency debate,
As into Red China she shot.
They sent up ballistic missiles,
To guide Granny Gertrude down,
While fashion experts in Paris,
Lavished praise on her naughty nightgown.

She careered through Vladivostok,
Without even a backward look,
And paused long enough in Bolivia,
To sign the visitors' book.
Then with one final triumphant leap,
Home to her cosy bed she hopped,
Having proved for all the world to see,
That determined Grannies just can't be stopped.

A BIT OF RHYME AND REASON

I found two squirrels in my top pocket,
And called them Henry and Millicent Sprockett,
       . . . because it rhymes.

When Henry and Millicent both said 'Please',
I found them tons of bread and cheese,
       . . . because it rhymes.

One day they both moaned 'We feel sick',
I gave them a spoon of arsenic,
       . . . because it rhymes.

The angry judge, his hammer banged,
And said: "At dawn you must be hanged,"
       . . . because it rhymes.

I merely said: "Fiddledy Dee",
And he was obliged to set me free,
       . . . because it rhymes.

A TIMELY WARNING

The next time you put 2 and 2 together,
Tie them up well with reinforced cord,
Or they'll produce such vulgar fractions,
That Maths will be banned by the Censorship Board.

THE STRANGE CASE OF NICODEMUS NOGGIN

Nicodemus Noggin was as precise as could be,
He counted his wife every day before tea,
'Till one fateful evening tho' he meant no offence,
He converted the answer to pounds, shillings and pence.

"I'm going home to mother" she said loud and clear.
He was too busy counting his left foot to hear.
After dividing the solution by the weight of a sneeze,
He multiplied his auntie by a half pound of cheese.
And following a sudden rush of porridge to his head,
He decimalised the crumbs from a loaf of stale bread.

So much mental work was a terrible strain,
Nicodemus developed a fraction on the brain,
He imagined himself to be all manner of things,
Like bus-stops, and budgerigars and wild Highland Flings.
He thought he was a telephone and became very ill,
When the Post Office cut him off for not paying the bill.
Then after standing for a day on one leg,
He laid a delightfully luminous egg.
"Farewell cruel world" was his last parting shout,
And imagining he was a candle, he blew himself out.

TIME AND TIDE

It was just the right job for a penguin with gout,
Making certain the tide came in, then went out.
'Till one day at midnight before noon could begin,
In spite of special magnets, the tide wouldn't come in.
The penguin consulted his book of French words,
And telephoned his granny who kept Mynah birds.
Granny was slightly deaf so the penguin had to shout,
"If the tide doesn't come in again, it can never go out!"
The old lady's hearing was terribly poor,
She said: "Mix in some flour and an egg to be sure."
Just then a field-mouse climbed up on a rock,
Dived into the sand and suffered severe shock.

First aid was rendered by a Knight of Malta flea,
Who sprayed it with sugar then passed round the tea.
The field mouse was taken to an intensive care ward,
Where doctors tickled nurses to avoid being bored.

After a week of raw turnips and a meadow of wheat,
The fieldmouse was better and back on its feet.
Meanwhile the penguin was in a terrible state,
For the tide was now seven days and two minutes late.
He telephoned his granny and yelled: "What'll I do?"
"Try six parts of semolina to three parts of glue."

Now please read this carefully wherever you are,
If you wish to help the penguin in his desperate hour,
Just fill up your bath and washbasin with water,
And pull out the plug at about half past a quarter.
The tide will come rushing back up the beach,
And the penguin will include YOU in his thanksgiving
    speech.

YOU ARE NOW ENTERING BALLYMAGOLD

You'll find very strange men in Ballymagold,
Who set fire to their trousers whenever it's cold.
Sometimes they wear coal scuttles on their heads,
To avoid being concussed by low-flying single beds.
They queue at antique shops to buy hot buttered toast,
Which they send to Archbishops by registered post.
The wives seldom gossip — there just isn't time,
What with husbands to embroider and chimneys to climb.
At weekends they gallop on a chauffeur driven horse,
With a retired sea-captain to plot out the course.
Weekdays are kept free for abducting millionaires,
And spacing them out in near perfect squares.
Ballymagold invites yourself to call in anytime,
A very cunning plot indeed to make this ending rhyme.

YOU CAN TELL BY LOOKING AT IT

This poem has no beginning,
It also has no end,
We might just get a middle in,
With a squeeze, a shove and a bend.

PECULIARLY PILKINGTON

Pilkington never wore a hat on his head,
He preferred to wear a ham omelette instead,
His right leg was insured against flood, fire and theft,
While a vigilant budgie protected his left.
He hunted rice pudding with an elephant gun,
And was once badly mauled by a wild currant-bun.
He wrestled single-handed with a savage meringue,
And perfected the world's very first silent bang.

Sometimes he lived inside Grandfather clocks,
And had his summer residence in a telephone box.
Pilkington was simply amazed by the fuss,
When he travelled upstairs on a single-decker bus.
It affected him so deeply that he married his wife,
And decided to lead a quiet, normal life,
So now when he finds that there's nothing to do,
He repairs old age pensioners with sticky tape and glue.

POINT TO PONDER

If men were mice and mice were men,
Pussy cats and women would have to think again.

MY RELATIVES WERE MILDLY DISTURBED

It's certain few have ever lived,
Like Uncle Nathaniel Wintergreen,
Who hung his wife on the garden line,
And brought her grapes at Hallow'een.

And there was never such a man,
As Uncle Henry Willington-Blink,
Who wore his dentures upside down,
And entertained in the kitchen sink.

One man who is quite unique,
Is the Honorable Walter Baltimore,
Who slept upstairs in a violin case,
And always snored 'till half past four.

But surely this man stood alone,
Old Cousin Billy Blessington-Brown,
Who sometimes hid in sacks of flour,
And hung lanterns in his dressing gown.

ECONOMY

Only eight words are contained in this line,
The way they pay poets, I couldn't afford nine.

DURING SHOCK TREATMENT

This poem solemnly asserts the sacred right of each and every Irish Duck to complete freedom of Quacks whenever each and every Irish duck feels so inclined.

The National League for Peace and for Quiet,
is launching a remarkable scheme
to De-Quack every duck in the land
with the Patent De-Quacking Machine.

"You plug in your duck
to our new Quack-Extractor",
says a spokesman for N.L.P.Q.,
"then gently tap his head with a mallet,
or a clout with a spanner will do.
As soon as your duck is soundly asleep
you press button E marked 'Extract';
the second his tail gives a spasmodic twitch,
he's been well and truly de-quacked."

Already the ducks are planning a rally,
with banners and slogans and chants;
they hope to find the appropriate Minister,
and Beakify the seat of his pants.
'Give us this day our daily quack,'
they've had it tattooed on their chests,
while the National League for P and for Q,
are still going ahead with their tests.

Now is the time for Irishmen to cry 'Halt',
this is not why we part with our tax;
something is lost to a nation for ever;
a tradition is as strong as its quacks.

The whole trouble with the civilised world is that we don't think before we empty the bath.

The spiders who live down your plughole
are always being soaked to the skin;
they build little hydro-electrical dams,
but the bathwater still gurgles in.

Some of them wear plastic goggles
to keep the soap out of their eyes;
old spiders wrap up in waterproof shawls,
young spiders damp-proof their thighs.

The spiders who live down your plughole
have arthritic elbows and knees;
some have got chills in their kidneys,
Others — an asthmatic wheeze.

Even their winter woollies are damp,
they're never cosy or snug;
as soon as they hang up the washing,
somebody pulls out the plug.

The spiders who live down your plughole
are anxious and tense to the core,
never knowing the day nor the hour
they'll all be washed down the shore.

Thank God for spiders in plugholes,
so, spider, hold up your head;
if you didn't live down our plugholes,
we'd have earwigs and beetles instead!

**This poem is respectfully dedicated to everybody
who secretly dreams of doing something outrageous,
like keeping traffic-wardens in a goldfish bowl, or
wallpapering their local greengrocer.**

Anyone who meets Fitzwilton O'Toole
agrees that he's not the same man;
he never used to gallop ponies upstairs,
and no one quite credits his plan
to drop hippopotami
from the top of the Alps
to see if hippopotami bounce.
Fitzwilton O'Toole never did things like that,
or auctioned his wife by the ounce.

Anyone who knows Fitzwilton O'Toole
is sadly shaking their heads;
he never used to fling bishops from trees,
or lock reverend mothers in sheds.
Even his close friends have to admit
his behaviour is strangely erratic;
nobody normal swings by his teeth
from the ballcock up in the attic.

An eminent psychiatrist places the blame
on his early days in the home;
his parents played ice-hockey in bed,
his mother wrote part of this poem.

But grieve not for Fitzwilton O'Toole,
you'll never hear him complain;
Fitzwilton has a radical theory —
the rest of the world is insane.

You have probably never met Macadoodle and for that reason may be inclined to dismiss him lightly which is a sorry indictment on the times in which we live and does not augur well for the future.

Macadoodle was born with a beard on his chin
and a fistful of liquorish pipes.
He was wearing two figleaves strategically placed,
and a hair piece with vertical stripes.

The midwife said medical history was made
while tucking him in for the night.
Macadoodle expertly rolled a cigar,
and said: "Madam, hast thou got a light?"

The christening was a dignified, joyous affair,
Macadoodle weighed sixteen stone ten.
The vicar suffered severe muscle strain,
he will never play hockey again.

Macadoodle's mother was patting his back,
"Has my baba got bold windy pains?"
Rhino stampeded, cathedrals collapsed,
and grown men were hurtled down drains.

Some say Macadoodle's in heaven,
some say he's paying for his sins,
but his mother and father say one simple prayer,
"Thank God Macadoodle wasn't twins!"

Malachy Grindlington-Grout may never go anywhere, but did it ever occur to you that he probably has a perfectly good reason!

Do you know Malachy Grindlington-Grout?
Do you know why he never comes out?
Some people say he's afraid that the rain
will trickle down his ears
and gurgle in his brain.

Others think he's scared that the sun
will sparkle up his nose
and melt every one
of his Christmas tree candles.
Do you know Malachy Grindlington-Grout?
Do you know why he never comes out?

Have you seen Malachy Grindlington-Grout?
Have you heard what the man is about?
Some people say he trains monster ants
to march in next door
and munch potted plants.

Others swear his cellar is full
of wild vestal virgins
so life won't be dull
in the long winter evenings.
Have you seen Malachy Grindlington-Grout?
Do you know why he never comes out?

A highly significant week in the growth, development and integration of Fitzhenry.

Monday

The sky didn't fall on Fitzhenry
    today,
and nothing dropped out of his
    head,
nobody sprayed him with straw-
    berry jam,
and put him 'twixt slices of bread.

Tuesday

No-one upholstered Fitzhenry
    today,
or raffled his moveable parts;
person unknown didn't leap out
    of trees
and puncture his tummy with
    darts.

Wednesday

Fitzhenry felt faintly uneasy today
when donkies peered over his
    hedge,
and hummed little tunes from
    Mozart and Strauss;
Fitzhenry felt slightly on edge.

Thursday

The doctor said: "Three tablets
    six times a day
if you see them in black and in
    white,
but for donkies that shimmer
    and glow after dark,
take three tablets six times at
    night."

Friday

The sky fell on top of Fitzhenry
    today,

and spare parts dropped out of
    his head;
the doctor thinks it's a really
    good sign,
 . . . "the tablets are working,"
    he said.

Twenty-eight words with spaces between to stop them bumping into each other.

A caterpillar
used to spill'er
dinner,
a shaky spider
used to spill his
tea,
but nobody
could spill
the Nervous Neville
'cos Nervous Neville
spilt
the Irish Sea.

Lady Violet Netherington-Springs and the miscellaneous objects that are inclined to gather and cluster underneath her bed.

Lady Violet Netherington-Springs
sometimes wonders at the things
that hide and huddle underneath her bed,
but so long as they behave,
trim their toe-nails,
wash and shave,
nothing very much is ever said.

Lady Violet Netherington-Springs
has never seen the things
that hide and huddle underneath her bed,
but she hears them winding clocks,
grooming horses,
darning socks,
and she smells them baking home-made soda-bread.

Lady Violet Netherington-Springs
has no objection to the things,
that hide and huddle underneath her bed,
but now they're felling trees,
raising goats and keeping bees,
she feels it's time
that something firm was said.

Lady Violet Netherington-Springs
has reasoned with the things
that hid and huddled underneath her bed,
now she was gentle, kind and soft,
now they're all tucked in aloft,
and she hides and huddles underneath instead.

The back-to-front people of Orris-in-Bossory which sounds like Borris-in-Ossory, but isn't, so they can't take a legal action against me.

Those reversible folk of Orris-in-Bossory
don't back horses — they front them,
they're not very kind to Grandads and Grans,
the Orris-in-Bossories hunt them.
They pump warm milk into their cows,
and out comes pasteurised grass;
they stuff boiled eggs into their hens,
but not before administering gas.

Those reversible folk of Orris-in Bossory,
say 'Grace after Meals' before tea,
then 'Grace before Meals' comes after dinner,
and twins comes in batches of three.

The Back-to-Front folk of Orris-in-Bossory,
are impeccably dressed when they're born,
in stainless steel nappies, and stainless steel skin,
you can tell that it's hardly been worn.

If ever you go to Orris-in-Bossory,
don't get there until you come back,
for when you're leaving it's time to arrive,
so there's really no need to unpack.

They may be only a set of false teeth to you, but inside each and every tooth is an intense longing to be taken seriously and accorded the dignity that is its due.

This is the day no false tooth forgets,
the day he receives his degree.
Last night they confessed to Father False Tooth,
to prepare themselves spiritually.
Last night they went to bed bright and early,
but precious few of them slept;
they prayed in the silences of their souls,
and some of them quietly wept.
Tomorrow at the False Tooth Training Authority
all the Doctors of Dentures will be there
to salute each false 'tute' of the future:
Graduation is a solemn affair.
Until now it's been every tooth for himself,
each one has studied alone,
soaking in jamjars, side by side,
but each tooth was soaked on his own.
Tomorrow they parade in cap and in gown,
tomorrow each one of them gets
his official appointment . . . 'Upper' or 'Lower',
for the first time they'll form up in sets.
The Dean of the College will give them his blessing,
they'll recite the Divine Denture Code:
"We promise never ever to rattle,
not even when noses are blowed.
We promise never to choke anybody,
we'll never pop out when they laugh,
and when they chew their sticky toffee,
we won't look for 'Time and a Half'.
God bless you — false teeth of the future
we pray you will never forget
even the poshest of upper-class dentures
aren't better than the lower-class set.

It's a pity that more people don't socialise with the Bassington-Browns because they're really very nice when you get to know them.

(A poem containing elements of sociological significance).

People who visit the Bassington-Browns
never feel fully at ease
as Nigel Bassington whips off your socks
and Cynthia inspects you for fleas.

"Come in — do be seated," say the Bassington-Browns
as they hunt out the camels and yaks;
the penguin in the corner is supposed to be stuffed,
though he still munches trousers and slacks.

Conversation is difficult at the Bassington-Browns;
you'll find yourself groping for words
while they perch on the sideboard all flapping their arms,
and pretend to be tropical birds.

You'll never be bored at the Bassington-Browns,
especially if Grandad is there,
for he digs mighty tunnels from the local Town Hall,
and surfaces under your chair.

Sometimes Grandmother raises her crutch,
and a wild glint comes into her eye:
"It's time to be herding the bison," she says,
"I can sense them . . . they're grazing nearby."

After Granny springs onto her horse,
there's nothing much more to be done.
"Do call again," say the Bassington-Browns,
"We're here between a quarter-past one!"

It is not a good idea to become over-anxious about the relative positions of one's feet, nose and other optional extras. Worthington gave the matter too much thought and blew his ancillary gasket.

Worthington worried about the great distance
between his big toe and his brain
in case a message to waggle went astray,
and precipitated mild corset strain.

He worried because his nose was too near
to his thought-thinking cerebral place,
for fear a sudden impulse to sneeze
would blow it clean off his face.

He worried so much about his two legs
not receiving orders to walk
that he fitted his shins with an intercom system,
so if they got bored they could talk.

"Worthington calling my ear on the left,
if you're receiving me — wiggle!"
But communications were fast breaking down,
the right ear gave a slow, sluggish squiggle.

"Worthington Control to Grand Central Navel:
what is the position about fluff?"
But the navel never answered his call,
its transmitter was clogged with the stuff.

Worthington is re-designing his body.
His brain is where his tummy should be.
But where are his eyes? Oh do tell us, pray!
Well, should he sit down, he can't see!

This poem may appear to defame the character of the Squoshly-Pod Squirrels but if you were on the receiving end of one of their nuts, you'd have written it too.

The delinquent squirrels of Squoshly Pod
have got no respect for the law.
They puncture the tyres on pensioners' bikes,
with a marlin-spike clutched in each paw.

The ill-behaved squirrels of Squoshly Pod,
set fire to barristers' wigs,
then tie female juries to trees,
and bombard them with syrup of figs.

The probation officers of Squoshly Pod,
tried sending the squirrels to school.
They locked their teacher under the stairs,
and sauntered downtown to play pool.

Social workers have gone into the woods
and tried meaningful discussion,
but were pelted with boxes of seven stone nuts,
and emerged with suspected concussion.

Bishops and vicars — deacons and nuns —
are being drafted towards Squoshly Pod.
When all else fails with irreverent squirrels,
when all else fails — then try God!

A Grouchey Bird as a pet is not such a good idea as you may be inclined to think.

Keeping a Grouchey bird as a pet
is a very unnerving affair,
for he slides up the bannisters,
sleeps in the sink,
and has long lank lugubrious hair.

The Grouchey bird is an ill-mannered pet
who seldom says 'Thank you' or 'Please'.
He puts his feet on the table,
his elbows in the soup,
and never, ever, ever give him peas.

Grouchey Birds have no respect for the cloth,
they doze off to sleep during Mass,
stick their tongues out at bishops,
chase nuns around convents,
and snore during Pre-Marriage Class.

A Grouchey Bird is an ungrateful creature,
you'll find him asleep in your bed,
he'll drink all your toothpaste,
pour ink on your wife,
and place bottled gas on her head.

Whenever they hear a knock at the door,
they'll search for a place they can hide,
they'll dash up the chimney,
rush up your trousers;
Grouchies don't know the meaning of pride.

Do not keep a Grouchey Bird as a pet,
there's nothing more to be said.
Grouchey Birds do not eat their young,
they eat themselves instead.

Ig . . . a . . . natius !

Ig-a-natius had an unmerciful itch,
complete with a terrible catch.
It changed direction every time
Ig-a-natius attempted to scratch.

Sometimes it tickled around his leg,
and sometimes his fifty-mile-limit.
But whenever he tried to scratch it to death
it escaped before he could pin it.

When Ig-a-natius settled down for the night
he wriggled, he squirmed and he twitched.
His wife took to sleeping up telegraph poles,
she swore that her man was betwitched.

"You gave me your hand in marriage," she said,
"the same hand you now use to scratch it."
Then she posted herself to 'All Other Places',
for fear that she too might catch it.

Ig-a-natius was beside himself with grief,
but the itch was beside him as well.
He sprayed it with essence of six-inch nails,
but this itch had no sense of smell.

Some people won't give you the time of the day,
others wouldn't give you the itch.
Ig-a-natius offers you absolutely free,
his wriggle — his squirm — and his twitch.

It is considered profoundly inadvisable to go through life using words like 'sprunkle' . . . ridgy smoley' . . . and/or 'cring' because the greater mass of the populace won't have the faintest idea what you are talking about.

Mavis Metastopholes invented new words,
such as 'Sprunkle', 'Ridgy Smoley' and 'Cring'.
She never told anyone what the words meant,
but high in the rafters she'd sing:
"I will sell my soul for a half ton of Sprunkle,"
and menfolk queued up by the score,
with sackfuls of grindle and gallons of nerk,
but none of them got past her door.

"I will trade my heart for a moist ridgy smoley,
even though it be crumpled and worn,"
but even when one man brought essence of noole,
Mavis dismissed him with scorn.

One day Mavis' father said: "Go feed the grindles,
and enough of this nonsense you speak."
"BUT FATHER!" . . .too late . . . the man he was gone.
The girl was betwixt and betweak.

Mavis Metasopholes was swallowed by a grindle
with a flourish, a grunt and a croak. She tried to explain
. . . "Eh — Sprunkle and Cring,"
. . . the last words Metastopholes spoke.

The nearly extinct, but not quite, Trim Tummy Wobbling Tribe.

In the steaming jungles of tropical Trim,
where man-eating hamsters run free,
where wild, untamed blue-tits are thumping their chests,
and the breeze shakes the lumpy porridge tree —
that's where you'll find a curious tribe
which everyone thought was extinct:
the Trim Tummy Wobblers are alive and well,
they're aliver and weller than you thinked.
At sunrise they assemble their tummies;
each stomach is pointed due East
ready for the ceremonial wobble
to announce the lumpy porridge feast.
All eyes are fixed on the Chief Tummy Wobbler,
his stomach tattoed with plain chant,
for these are the mystical Tummy Wobbling Words,
without them . . . to wobble . . . you can't.
The Chieftain speaks the first sacred phrase,
"Tapioca, suet pudding, cold rice."
Then he rhythmically rumbles to the north and the south,
and Wibbles significantly . . . twice.
All of a sudden — it happens at once —
the tummies excitedly quiver.
The jungle is still,
the eyes are all closed,
you can feel a tingle and shiver.
The whole earth trembles,
monkies fall out of trees,
as tummies throb and gyrate;
the Trim Tummy Wobblers are praising the Lord,
for the lumps of porridge on each plate.
Then the wobbling is finished,
and so is the porridge,
how long they'll sleep — no one can tell,
resting their tummies — building up their strength,
for the wobble before dinner as well!

This poem may seem whimsical in content, but verily in sooth, the implications could well rock the very foundations of civilisations or whatever or possibly both.

The good Lord created the humble sardine,
complete with a fine set of fins.
The good Lord promised them heaven on earth,
but he never said nothing about tins.

Mankind has thwarted the great Divine plan,
mankind has grievously sinned.
Sardines were created to inherit the sea,
yet they all finish up being tinned!

Sardines have never broken the law,
they don't even swim three abreast.
They're always in bed before half-past-ten,
with a hot bottle clutched to their chest.

What have they done to deserve such a fate?
It's bad enough winding up dead.
But it's far worse again when you finish your days,
as special offer, cheap sardine spread.

Can you look a sardine straight in the face,
can you say your conscience is clear?
Let us become a truly human race,
so that sardines have nothing to fear.

Have you ever heard a sardine complain
about gross overcrowding within?
Yet the Ministry for Tinnery couldn't care less
how many are bunged in a tin.

Each of us must stand alone
when we reach the last Judgement place.
Each of us must answer for ourself.
"Can you look a sardine straight in the face?"

Contrary to public opinion, the Fidgety Folk of Fumbally Street are not 'work-shy' . . . it's just that they've got better things to be doing with their time.

(An Anthropological Study).

The fidgety folk of Fumbally Street,
are terribly awkward and clumsy.
They climb into their beds and miss;
these folk are all fingers and thumbsy.

Sometimes they don't have a weekend at all,
their calendar's a couple of days slow.
Their average height is 57 pence,
they invest themselves — that's how they grow.

The fidgety folk of Fumbally Street
all search one another for fleas;
they inspect second cousins for rising damp,
and structural faults in the knees.

Once every year in Fumbally Street,
they think about looking for work.
They look up their chimneys and under flat stones
and in swamps where it's likely to lurk.

For this is 'Fumbally-find-A-Job' Day,
when everyone searches their attics.
But Fumbally folk don't look very hard;
they claim that work gives them rheumatics.

On Sundays, Father Fumbally speaks,
"He who shuns work is a sinner."
Then he mentions a second collection for Share,
and they all stampede home for the dinner!

The law of the Church hath put a stop to Tweezle Enthwhistle's gallop, but not quite in the orthodox manner.

Tweezle Enthwhistle shouted bold words,
like 'trousers' and 'tummy' and 'legs'.
Tweezle Enthwhistle shocked mother birds;
he tied naughty things to their eggs.

Tweezle telephoned old maiden aunts
and told them their ears would drop off.
He said that the same would happen to their feet
the very next time that they cough.

He stuck out his tongue at vicars and nuns,
he locked 'My Lord Bishops' in sheds.
He pelted arch-deacons with curranty buns
and dropped Eccles cakes on their heads.

Tweezle heard that 'The end is nigh;
even now it may be too late!'
Confessions began at twenty past ten;
he was there at a quarter past eight.

Enthwhistle never really confessed;
he found something safer to do.
Somebody said: "The last shall be first,"
so he stayed at the end of the queue.

One may be strongly tempted to sit in self-righteous judgement on the scurrilous conduct of six thousand, seven hundred and thirty gnus, but it might be more advisable to put one's own house in order first.

(A Theosophical Meditation).

Six thousand, seven hundred and thirty gnus
hopped into bed for a snore and a snooze,
'till the Reverend Gnu came cycling upstairs,
and said: "Everyone out — you've forgotten your prayers!"

Six thousand, seven hundred and thirty gnus
grabbed woolly socks and snuggeldy shoes,
sprayed one another with warm anti-freeze,
hopped out of bed and on to their knees.

"Let us pray for less fortunate gnus,
sleeping on benches or locked into zoos,
for all gnus hungry and gnawing at bones,
and our brethren banned from Non-Gnu Zones."

Six thousand, seven hundred and thirty gnus
started to argue who's pillow was whose,
they belted each other with blunt bars of soap
while Reverend Gnu preached Faith, Love and Hope.

It would be all too easy to cast the first stone,
to insist that the sinner repent and atone,
but remember — before you accuse the gnus —
could you walk through this poem in their shoes?

The trouser legs of Mullingar South find complete fulfilment during their leisure time, and as a result are well-adjusted and not subject to negative impulses.

The trouser legs of Mullingar South
can't wait for the night-time to fall;
they're placed hanging up at the end of the bed,
or dangled from a nail on the wall.

As soon as their masters are soundly asleep
the trouser legs wait for the call
that comes from on high from Divine Trouser Leg,
while mice tremble down in the hall.

"Oh come all ye trousers,
the time it is nigh
to dance Highland Flings on the stairs
to slide down the bannisters,
hop, skip and jump,
to bounce up and down on the chairs."

The trousers legs of Mullingar South
tippitoe out the front door;
left legs and right legs keeping in step,
old trousers' proud spirit soar.

They march up the hillside
and chase mountain goats,
they stand on their left legs
and spin.
Young trousers chase after shy ladies' slacks,
though none of the young trousers sin.

Studious trouser legs study hard sums
and how to make soda-bread rise;
they hold secret ballots to see if the choice
is buttons or zips on their flies.

The moment the sun peeps over the trees
the trouser legs scamper for home;
nobody knows except you and me
the places where trouser legs roam.

Only one thing the trouser legs ask
of good folk whose thinking is right:
do not put a stop to their happy high-jinks,
don't lock up your trousers at night.

**It is sheer folly for an unmarried squirrel to confide
her innermost thoughts to another unless the trust
level is high and clearly defined.**

"Can you keep a secret?" asked Cynthia Squirrel,
"I promise" said Professor McGlynn,
"Well, myself and the boyfriend" said Cynthia Squirrel,
"Me and the boyfriend are living in sin."

"Can you keep a secret?" asked Professor McGlynn,
"Cross my heart" said Beatrice Von Bat,
"Well, Cyril and Cynthia Squirrel" he said,
"Are shacked up in cohabitat."

"Can you keep a secret?" asked Beatrice Von Bat,
"But of course" said Methusela Mole,
"Well, Cyril and Cynthia Squirrel" she said,
"Have mortal sin writ on their soul."

"Can you keep a secret?" asked Methusela Mole,
"Trust me" said Cecilia McCrow,
"Well Cyril and Cynthia Squirrel" she said,
"Aren't married, but they're . . . well, you know!"

No-one informed Cyril Squirrel,
His behaviour is naughty and bold,
And everyone's keeping his secret so well,
It seems like he'll never be told!

The Tallaght Tom-Cats All Male Voice Choir.

When old cats are snoring in hammocks,
and kittens tucked into their cots,
when grandmother tabbies talk in their sleep
of retirement on luxury yachts,
that's when the heavens are filled with a song
that seems to rise higher and higher,
night-watchmen find themselves singing along
with the Tallaght Tom-Cats Male Voice Choir.

Nagging wives suddenly fall silent,
burglars decide to go straight,
the whole world turns towards Tallaght,
the oil wells are hushed in Kuwait.
Then comes the harmonic howling,
they sing Verdi with passionate fire,
then "Onwards Christian Pussies,"
the Tallaght Tom-Cats Male Voice Choir.

Holy men perching on bus-stops,
hairy men sitting up trees,
squirrels sucking their cough drops,
and mice making omelettes with cheese;
suddenly all of them silent,
as it echoes through the night,
a message with infinite feeling —
"Pussy cats of the world — unite."

Some say they find the strength to go on,
others the faith they had lost,
some say the meaning of life becomes clear —
count your blessings
and don't count the cost.
While out on the South-side of Dublin,
accompanied by harp, lute and lyre,
they also whistle, yodel and lilt,
that versatile Tallaght All Male Voice Choir.

**A stuffed bird is all very well under certain
circumstances, but it is no substitute for a plump plover.**

It's a fear that's felt by few,
just a handful ever knew
what was suffered
by Demetrius O'Shea.
for he lived in mortal dread,
of things landing on his head,
and erecting homes with twigs
and sticks and clay.

Whenever walking out of doors,
he did sometimes spring down shores,
but only when things circled for a landing.
Like roast duck with brussels sprouts,
or pheasants seasoned out,
homeless birds can be selfishly demanding.

Demetrius wore a sign,
a Celtic carved design,
to let birds know
exactly where they stood:
"Thou shalt not attempt to land,
loiter, linger, dance or stand."
He insured the head,
for fire and theft and flood.

But life can really bore you,
when your feathered friends ignore you;
not a winged thing to prance upon your dome.
Demetrius O'Shea
began to slowly wilt away;
he regretted ever entering
this poem.

'Tis a lonely desolate sight,
a head — deserted day and night;
we say O'Shea has got himself to blame.
He tried a grey stuffed owl,
and other artificial fowl,
but birds with stuffing simply aren't the same.

Nosey neighbours know

Geoffrey Addington-Spratt with grace,
Ballet danced on a fillet of plaice,
In vain his neighbours tried to trace,
His green and yellow tablets.

Geoffrey Addington-Spratt divine,
Lassoed himself with a ball of twine,
Neighbours blamed it on the wine,
And his green and yellow tablets.

Geoffrey Addington-Spratt with ease,
Roller skated up sycamore trees,
Neighbours said: "You've forgotten these,
Your green and yellow tablets."

Geoffrey Addington-Spratt at seven,
Assumed himself straight into heaven,
Neighbours blamed it on the leaven,
In his green and yellow tablets.

A sort of solution to the hopsididdle problem

Supposing that a hopsididdle
decided to live under the bed,
Hopsididdles sleep all day
and play bagpipes at night instead
of sleeping.
Supposing that the hopsididdle
moved in his family as well,
Hopsididdles throw hedgehogs at each other
and nobody can tell
the day nor the hour
that they heat tax inspectors
with blowlamps.

You can always keep a tame
Hen-dem-nya-biddy-cup
in your bedroom.
Hopsididdles are terrified of them.
Hen-dem-nya-biddy-cups eat people
in nighties and pyjamas though
so they are really only
a very temporary solution.
It might be better in the long run
to put up with having hedgehogs thrun
by unruly hopsididdles
than a statement on your tombstone
which says "Cut off in his prime
by a very hungry Hen-dem-nya-biddy-cup.

Do you give up?
Better men than you did
to be suddenly eaten alive
by a ravenous
Inta-minta-poppa-tinta-tooma-tomma-tossa.
God alone knows where THAT came from.

Ponsonby's Christmas

Peace on Earth,
Good will to all men,
means nothing to Ponsonby-Warner,
He illuminates his wife with 50,000 volts,
and stands her in a tub in the corner.

"Gloria in Excelcis Deo",
sing the carollers outside his door,
Ponsonby-Warner crouches on the roof,
They never sing an encore.
Ponsonby aims his Christmas Pudding Launcher,
And lets fly with sultanas and suet,
then a lethal burst of mixed candied peel,
Gallantly they try to sing through it.

"Once in Royal David's City",
That's as far as they got,
Ponsonby loosed off his Minced Pie Missiles,
And each pie was minced piping hot.
Some of the carollers sprang into lakes,
Others scrambled up trees,
One of them stunned by a flying sultana,
Marched off to Mass on his knees.

"Peace on Earth
Good will to all men,"
Those sentiments can't mean a thing.
To a man who sprays his granny with sparkle,
and suspends her with giftwrapping string.

Let us pray for Ponsonby-Warner,
That the meaning of Christmas becomes clear,
Let us pray for Ponsonby's wife,
With a bulb flashing out of each ear.
Finally . . . a whispered prayer for his granny,

All tied up with sparkles and string,
. . . Ponsonby-Warner . . . listen very closely,
Hark . . . the Herald Angels sing . . .

The Feast of Nicholas Von Noo

'Twas on the feast of Nicholas Von Noo,
All the people were facing due west,
Waiting for a Von Nooish vision to appear,
they all knew that Von Noo is truly blessed.

Twenty past Tuesday, the glow did gloo,
the bretheren emitted ragged cheers,
Old ladies brandished their husbands aloft,
Bus inspectors clipped each others ears.

Nicholas Von Noo did shimmer in the sky,
All our wrongs did strangely come to rights,
Prices spiralled downwards, strikers all unstruck,
And runs unran themselves in ladies tights.

Imitation fur coats were honest and mewed,
Hairpieces grew and grew and grew,
Till one little girl did sniffle and did snuff,
And said: "I don't believe in Nick Von Noo."

All the people fought mad religious wars,
"For Nicholas", "For Von" and "For Noo",
The little girl watched a daffodil grow,
And wondered at the things that grown-ups do.

Persons who never teach badgers to balance on each other's shoulders are strangely uncomfortable in the presence of people who do.

The man who lived in Flat Number Nine,
Seldom stepped outside his door,
But persons with donkeys called in to see him,
And galloped around on his floor.

The woman who lived in the flat underneath,
Wakened far into the night,
To the thunder of hooves and the roaring of crowds
And the swishing of bodies in flight.

The man who lived in Flat Number Nine,
Never got phone calls or post,
But farmers with charolais called in to see him,
He fed them warm winkles on toast.

The man who lived in Flat Number Nine,
Didn't trouble the rest of the house,
He always alerted them well in advance,
Before hunting wild pheasants and grouse.

Everyone else tried staying in their rooms,
But were bored in a matter of hours,
The man in Flat Nine fiddled and sang,
And hummed little tunes to red flowers.

They signed a petition to have him thrown out,
"the man has a problem" they said.
"It's for his own good. It's all for the best",
And at half nine they all went to bed.

The nudge equalisers shall inherit the world

Barnaby Squires packed up his comb
and a crateful of chocolate fudge,
"I'm going on an expedition" he said,
"To equalise the nudge."

He negated several hurdles
He dismantled a second-hand spludge,
But his mind ne'er strayed
From the plans he'd made,
To equalise the nudge.

Barnaby Squires searched high and low,
He scouted far and wide,
He unwound several Wimples,
And slid them down a slide.

The sun was setting in the west,
Burnishing quagmires of sludge,
Barnaby took no rest in his quest,
To equalise the nudge.

To the top of mountain peaks he climbed,
He walked on the ocean bed,
Where'eer he walked or climbed or swam,
These indomitable words he said.

"What matter if you strive and fail,
What matters is you tries it,
So seek and find and catch your nudge,
And boldly equalise it."

Metalurgists stopped metalurging,
Mechanics ceased to mechan,
Newly weds left their double beds,
To follow this singular man.

Cross-town traffic ground to a halt,
Budgies were unwilling to budge,
The civilised world and his wife had gone,
To equalise the nudge.

When life seems unworth the living,
When you dread the coming of day,
Look yourself straight in the face,
And with quiet conviction say:

"What matter if I strive and fail,
What matters is I tries it,
I shall seek and find my nudge,
And boldly equalise it!"

AFTER SHOCK TREATMENT

THE NIGHT THEY HANGED TEN DOGS
IN DINGLE

A little girl told the man.
She looked at him and she said
"A woman hanged ten dogs
in the house where
you're sleeping tonight.
Then she drowned herself."

An Americal girl told the man.
She looked at him and she said
"Take my hand and squeeze it —
then kiss me."
So he asked her — "I suppose
you never hanged ten dogs
and drowned yourself."
She shook her head.
So he took her hand
and he squeezed it.
And he kissed her.
Then she said it.
"My mother did though —
in the house where
you're sleeping tonight."

The man who owned the house told him
He looked at him and he said.
"I caught 27 salmon in my nets once
but a seal ate every one of them.
He pulled them through the net
headfirst and swallowed them."

The man who owned the house
gave him a plastic dish
with 15 crabs legs in it.
Then he gave him a spoon.
"Crack the legs open with that"
he said. "And eat what's inside."

So he asked him — "Are you married
to the American girl whose mother
hanged the dogs?"
"No — I'm not."
So he ate the crabs legs.
Then the man said it.
"No I'm not — but my brother is.
He's in the room next to you
in the house where you're sleeping tonight."

The man with the hole in his shoe
who rings the church bells told him.
He looked at him and he said.
"There's a shovel. Dig a hole
and stand in it. I'll ring
the church bells while you're digging."
So he asked him — "How deep will I dig?"
"Take out enough clay to bury a house
and muffle the howling of ten dogs."
The man with the hole in his shoe rang the bells.
And he dug.

The little girl told the man.
She looked at him and she said.
"Somebody buried the house
where you were sleeping last night
and I was only joking about the dogs
— honestly I was.

And the woman never drowned herself.
But somebody buried her in the house
last night and her American daughter
and the man she married and his brother.
And there's a huge grave all freshly dug
and the church bells are ringing —
that's my father ringing them now."

The man left town with his hands
in his pockets the way that nobody
would see the clay under his fingernails.

The little girl went home
and brought her father's ten dogs
out for a walk.

WHERE ARE YOU ALL HIDING?

Some people die
without ever having owned
a colour television
a car
a fridge
a stereo
a video
a detached residence
a set of golf clubs
a food blender
      grinder
      nebuliser
      mincer
      shredder
      liquidiser.
I'd love to know where
you are right now.
I want to meet you.
We've got a lot of what
we haven't got in common.

TONIGHT THEY PUT THE COTSIDES UP

Tonight they put the cotsides up
onto the old man's bed,
"You can't fall out and hurt yourself"
that's what the nurses said.
And God you should have seen it,
you should have seen his face,
as metal sides both rattled
and bolts clanked into place.

He sat there numb
and silent,
silent
and very very still,
and nobody who saw him,
nobody ever will
forget the way the colour
drained right out of his face,
as metal sides both rattled
and bolts clanked into place.

The nurses said the cotsides
were to keep him safe in bed,
"You can't fall out and hurt yourself,"
that's what the nurses said.
The rest of us lay looking,
we know that no matter how far
that old man fell in future
it could never leave a scar
the way those cotsides did.

Nobody wanted to catch his eye,
he was curled up silent and still,
maybe he'll go asleep for us,
that's it — maybe he will
go asleep embraced in a cradle,
in the morning they'll take
the sides down,

Go asleep embraced in a cradle,
that's the way Jesus was found.

You couldn't go over and talk to him,
for that would only mean . . .
you couldn't go over and talk to him
for then you'd have to lean
and look in over the top,
nobody wanted to do that,
remind him of the way you'd stop
and gaze at a new born infant.
And merciful God you couldn't peep,
peeping through the bars would be worse,
You couldn't go over and talk to him,
softly he started to curse,
"Do yez think I'm a bloody baby,
Do yez think I'm a baby or what?"
then he sank down under the covers,
in between the sides of his cot.

Tonight they put the cotsides up,
onto the old man's bed,
You can't fall out and hurt yourself,"
that's what the nurses said.
The rest of us lay looking,
we knew that no matter how far
that old man fell in future
it could never leave a scar
the way those cotsides did.

A SALUTE TO THE CONNEMARA CAP MAN

Craggy Connemara men,
Grey grey wisps of hair
and then the brown and grey
and grimy cap,
front pulled down nose to peak
the way you'd seldom sneak
a look into his eyes.
He peers down
to see into his pint,
never sees straight ahead
unless his neck is tilted back
and that is only when the crack
is ninety and sure then you'd
have to be looking anyway.

Never take it off.
Let the doctor X-ray you through it,
Never take it off unless say
a gale force nine blew it,
Sure then you might never get it back,
And that'd be a black day
for a craggy Connemara cap man.
Never take it off unless alone
or surrounded by other fully grown
consenting Connemara cap men.
They know what's underneath,
They've looked in mirrors.
A head that's baby's bottom white,
You'd see it on the darkest night,
A boon for any wife
Who's looking for the bed
with the light switched off.

A funeral or a lady or a priest
was the only time you'd ever lift it.
The only other thing
that would regularly shift it

was an act of God
and that was Mass on Sunday.
God bless you Connemara cap men,
We shall never see your likes again
and more's the pity,
All we ever saw in the city
was the coalman with his cap on
front to back
and to the Connemara cap man
gan aon doubt ar bith,
that was not the crack.

IT'S ALL RIGHT AS LONG AS THEY SAY IT

Everybody told him.
"You're great . . .
You are great."
Everywhere he went
they told him.
"Ooooh yeeeaaah . . .
Y . . . O . . . U . . .
A . . R . . . E . . .
GRRREEEAAATTT!!"
So he climbed to the top
of the highest mountain
and he shouted it . . .
"I . . . AM . . . GREAT!!!"

"Who the fuck does he think he is?"
That's what they said.
And everyone threw rocks at him
Until he was decently dead.

MORE ALIVE

Why?
They're crying.
"Dead."
They keep saying it.
"He's dead,
Why did he die?"
I have never felt better
in my what?
All that bone and hair
and skin . . .
Me?
That?
Aw listen. They're
saying it again.
"Why did he die?"
That thing. Not me. Lump.
That thing is going down
and down and down until
the earth comes up around it.
Thump. Thump.
Clump on a box.
It isn't me . . . lump,
I'm up here . . . see —
Oh no — you can't.
Through the wall,
Inside a drop of dew,
Sitting on a brown moth's wing,
Up and down
and in and out
and being a part of anything
you care to mention.

Vapour . . . that too,
seaspray
Hey — over here!
The sunbeam,
too slow — you missed me!
God — you're so slow
and heavy and bone and skin,
I've been to there and back
in the time you take
to crack your finger.

Are you coming to the funeral?
You know — the burial of thing.
Don't forget to bring
some flowers.
Don't forget to look
Up and far
and up and over
the edge of the world.
You won't see me
but you might see
where I've just been
or was or did or could
and this too will be yours.
More dead than alive
is back to front,
if this is being deceased
I'm sorry you can only
do it once . . .

THE BIRDS ARE SMOKING

Eh no — the birds — they don't sing anymore.
Oh yes — I know they used to.
With glorious song they used to pour their hearts out.
Round about dawn, the way you'd yawn
And leap out of bed
With your heart and your head
Full of glorious birdsong.
But now, you see, they're smoking,
Thrushes and sparrows and robins,
The birds are smoking 40 cigarettes a day,
Listen . . . listen to the parrot say —
"Pretty Polly — have you got a light?"
And far into the night
All the birds are wheezing,
And one or two of them might
Just sing for you tomorrow morning
But I doubt it.

Hey — now it's dawn,
Listen — the birds are yawning,
And here it comes — what used to be
A lovely early morning sound,
Listen — all around, the birds
are spluttering and gasping and choking,
Because you see — the birds are smoking.

Yes — I know — I know they used to fly,
Soaring up and down
and gliding on high
But now the birds don't fly much any more.

They haven't got the breath or the puff,
One little flutter of their wings is enough
To wear a robin out,
He has to rest now
After flying from one bough to another.
And do you remember how

The swallows used to fly away to Africa?
At summer's end off they'd go,
Well no — they don't do it anymore.
If they even flew to Farranfore in Kerry
They'd be flat on their backs
Trying to get their breath,
The birds are smoking themselves to death.

Excuse me Mr Blackbird,
I'd like to hear you sing.
What? You'd have to take off your oxygen mask?
Excuse me Mr Robin,
Why is it that you gasp
And choke and splutter,
Oh — I see — it's because the birds are smoking.

Sing a song of cigarettes,
A pocket full of smoke,
Four and twenty blackbirds
Cough and wheeze and choke,
When the pie was opened,
The birds began to gasp,
I've never seen a sight so sad,
As a bird in an oxygen mask.

Whenever I go into a small country pub a sort of silence falls and people wonder.

Tick tock, pub clock,
Whisper, whisper,
Look look quick look
When they think that
I'm not look look looking.
Look again
Avert the eye
Any time that I look
The way they're looking.

Maybe I'm a spy
Or better still
I might be going to rob the bank,
May God be thanked for the excitement.

Then they say
"I've probably come a long long way,"
"It's not such a bad oul day,"
Now that tongues have been found,
Thank God for the sound
Of people talking once again
The way that people do,
Before the stranger came through,
And brought it down to
Tick tock, pub clock,
Whisper Whisper,
"Who was that man on a white horse?"
It wasn't me,
I only came in
to do a wee
before the bus left for Achill.

THE FAMILY THAT FRIES TOGETHER
DIES TOGETHER

Yen San Chun and his wife
and child
died as they had lived.
Together.
It was better that way.
None of them to live
and look and see the others
fried.
Yen San didn't see
his brown and red and blackened
scorched beloved.
Arms fused into forehead
fused into the floor.
His son was more
like someone grilled
upon a spit
than someone killed
upon a hit
that was Hiroshima.

Yen San's wife was
with another child
and many a one
died because
its mother fried
around it.

Yen San's father saw his shadow
like some porcupine obscene.
His flesh in ribbons ripped
and standing up in strips unclean
like spines of porcupine.
Suddenly no longer father
husband or grandfather
to anyone except to pieces charred.
Already brown and black and hard

and harder still amongst the
kill and kill and kill
that was Hiroshima.

And still the sun came up
and still the sun went down
for seventy thousand "Yous"
and seventy thousand "Mes"
who never thought they'd
ever live to see it.
You and me and you
and me and you
and me.
Together in today.
A finger flick away
from Hiroshima.

GOD BLESS YOUR EYESIGHT

You told me
that you saw
the kitchen chairs
marching down
the garden path
to trample the life
out of the chrysanthemums.
I believe you.
After all
you're the only person
who has ever seen
anything in your
husband.

THAT'S NICE

He arranged his face into a nice expression
and approached the bus stop with the absolute
certainty that it would be there.
And by God — it was.
He said — "Good morning" to all the other people
with nice faces.
Nobody said — "What's good about it?"
They all said — "Good morning" to him.
And he said — "Good morning" to each of them.
"Nice day."
Nobody said — "What's nice about it?"
Everybody agreed that the day was nice,
and it was nice yesterday and with the help of God
it might be nice again tomorrow.
Then the bus came.
Everybody said — "Good morning" to the conductor.
. . . but he wasn't nice.
"What's good about it?"
He didn't say that.
But he thought it.
And that's not nice.
The day was.
Everybody had agreed on that.
But he wasn't.
They didn't say that.
That wouldn't be nice.
But they thought it.
And that's not nice.
That's bloody horrible.

The wild tangle-haired old man
with the sun-blackened face
and spit on his lips,
who wasn't going to work
and hadn't got the fare
and told the conductor
that his address was

"Number one — the great outdoors."
He said to me before I said
anything to him —
"If I was swept up in one of them
whirly cyclone twister yokes
that lifts houses up in the air —
do you know what I'd do?
I'd dance a hornpipe inside it
and God only knows where I'd land."

Please let me dance with you
inside your cyclone twister yoke.
We could whirl crazily around
and shout to people as they
hurtled past in their madly
spinning houses.
"That's a nice day."
And they'd roar back —
"What's nice about it?"
And we could have a real conversation.
Cyclones are great for that sort of thing.

SISTER FOUR COURSE

Some nuns take a vow of poverty
and eat in the Gresham Hotel.
Their name is not Mother Teresa.

FOR RITA WITH LOVE

You came home from school
on a special bus
full of people
who look like you
and love like you
and you met me
for the first time
and you loved me.
You love everybody
so much that it's not safe
to let you out alone.
Eleven years of love
and trust and time for you to learn
that you can't go on loving like this.
Unless you are stopped
you will embrace every person you see.
Normal people don't do that.
Some normal people will hurt you
very badly because you do.

Cripples don't look nice
but you embrace them.
You kissed a wino on the bus
and he broke down and he cried
and he said "Nobody has kissed me
for the last 30 years."
But you did.
You touched my face
with your fingers and said
"I like you."

The world will never
be ready for you.
Your way is right
and the world will
never be ready.
We could learn everything

that we need to know
by watching you
going to your special school
in your special bus
full of people
who look like you
and love like you
and it's not safe
to let you out alone.
If you're not normal
there is very little hope
for the rest of us.

CAN YOU HEAR IT?

I'm lying in the dark,
listening to a dog,
bark bark barking
in the far off.
Barking so that someone
will come and say
"There there my pet —
everything's alright."
I wish that someone
would come and say
that to me.
If I start bark barking,
the girl in the next flat
will surely ring the landlord.
He won't say "There there my pet."
I'm lying in the dark,
listening to a dog,
bark bark barking
in the far off.

IMPASSE

Eh — I wonder could I please
if it's not too much trouble,
like — if you're not run off your feet
or up to your eyes doing anything else,
could I have the Spaghetti Bolognese
when you're ready of course . . . please?

"Spaghetti's off!"

Oh — well in that case
if you could possibly manage it,
let me see now . . . I think
it'll be a toss-up between the . . .

"They're both off!"

Right — well — first things first,
I'll make a start with . . .

"Soup's off!"

Eh . . .

"That's off!"

Chef's Special.

"He's just shot himself!"

Glass of water.

"Tap's frozen!"

Your phone number.

"Cut off!"

Sex on top of the table.

"Legs are unsafe!"

On the floor then.

"Frighten the mice! . . . ."

Anywhere you suggest.

"Private suite in the Gresham
with a five course meal and
a bottle of champagne in a bucket!"

Tonight?

"Tonight's off!"

Tomorrow then?

"I'm working!"

After work?

"I have another job!"

Look — here's my diary,
you fill in the date.

"My pen's gone dry!"

All things considered
there is only one possible
solution to this absolute
impasse.

"Yes?"

At your earliest convenience,
when you have a second to spare,
and it fits in with your present arrangements . . .
kindly ----- off!

THE EYE-TO-EYER

An Eye-to-Eyer will always agree,
you can tell him
that black is white.
Now suddenly change
to black is black,
and he'll say — "By God
but you're right."

Eye-to-Eyers hate direct questions,
"Would you like china or delph?"
"Well that all depends,
eh — a wee bit of both,
like, what ever you're having yourself."

"WILL YOU HAVE COFFEE OR WILL YOU HAVE TEA?"
"I'll have whichever you make."
"IT'S NO TROUBLE — WHICH ONE DO YOU WANT?"
"I always get what I take."
"WELL, HOW ABOUT COFFEE?"
"That'll be grand."
"OR TEA?"
"A cup in me hand."

Eye-to-Eyers seldom take risks,
they're cautious in things that they say,
they wait till the heavens are bucketing down,
and they call it — "A damp sort of day."

An Eye-to-Eyer can't even choose,
between going to Heaven or Hell,
which makes it sort of awkward for God
and it's hard on the devil as well.

They do save the Lord a whole lot of work,
when it comes to their very last breath,
he doesn't have to pull out the plug
they bore one another to death.

FOR MY FATHER

It was raining
The day we buried my father.
Sleeting,slanting, freezing rain
In the cold-stone, wind-blown graveyard.
You always wanted to be buried here
In Malahide, not three miles further out.
There's room beside you still
For my mother.
You bought a double plot
So they would not
Bury my mother three miles further out.
Me and Ben carried the front
Of the highly polished box
With the shiny handles
And the men with the black caps
Supported the back.
Da — I was afraid I'd let you fall,
You were very very heavy.
We were proud and we were sad
To be carrying you.
Kevin Browne had dug a hole,
Tom, your brother said the prayers,
And the black umbrellas
Murmured the responses.
I hoped we'd stand forever
In the rain, beside the hole
and never leave you in your box.

But then we said the last Amen
And down you went.
Home we went
And still I see your hands
Cold and white.
Very white and very very cold.
Once they dug the soil,
But never no more.
Tandy your dog

Is lying at home
Watching the door,
He knows at 9 o'clock
Like every night before,
You'll take him
Up the road,
But never — never no more.

BIOLOGY LESSON

I am very very lonely today.
I can feel it in the pit of my stomach.
At this moment there are many people
who feel exactly the same way.
That's an awful lot of stomachs.
If we can all get together and talk about it
our stomachs will feel significantly better.
Or, we can remain in isolation
and talk to our stomachs.
"Dear stomach — I'm sorry you feel that way.
What you need is another stomach to relate to."

But hell — I can't approach a complete stranger
and say: "Excuse me — my stomach would like to
relate to yours."
I had thought about removing my shirt
and encouraging my stomach to relate
to itself in a mirror.
But that's the sort of behaviour that
brought down Sodom and Gomorrah.
I'm afraid there's only one thing for it.
Eh — if you'll show me in your stomach
I'll show you mine.

ALL YOU NEED IS LOVE

Old man wearing Beatle boots,
Stretched out sound asleep
in warming Glasgow city sun.
Doesn't see or hear
the fearful rush hour rushing rush,
Doesn't wash or brush or polish anything.
Someone shot John Lennon.
Beatles long since gone
singing over the top
into golden middle age,
but yours is olden and you smell.
Someone gave you Beatle boots,
so well they might
or perhaps they threw them out.
Lying on the grass is free
but icy cold at night.
Litter bins are three a penny
you don't have any place to go
when the sun's gone in
and all the rush hour people
cosy sit at home watching
today's answer to John,
Paul, George and Ringo.
Yesterday's answer to nothing at all
wakens with the evening chill,
all you need is love.
But where's the lover?
Who will give it to you?

Love is all you need,
not rundown wornout Beatle boots,
thrown away by yesterday's
beautiful people.
You're beautiful
and grey
and somebody will surely
phone an ambulance

the day you need it.
John Lennon got one too.

THE INJUSTICE OF IT ALL

"Excuse me" she said
"Is this seat taken?"
I shook my head and
the woman sat down.
She placed a tin box
in front of her and opened it.
Twenty three very hungry spiders
marched across the table
and surrounded my plate.
She clicked her fingers
and they demolished my dinner.
"One word out of you" she said,
"And they'll eat you as well."
When she had gone
I told a waitress that I wished
to complain to the manager.
"I'm sorry sir" she said,
"The spiders ate him last night."
If that is so, I don't understand
why they were still so hungry.
Somebody is lying through their teeth.
I explained all of this
to a woman on the bus
and she said: "Are you from
outer space or what?"
There's nothing the matter with me.
I don't carry spiders around in a tin box.
I might be better off if I did.

I'M LOOKING AT YOU

Lovely, lazy, laid-back,
nice and easy, cool
as a casual couldn't care less,
you'd never guess
and that's the whole idea.

Woo woo — more relaxed than you,
never up to ninety
about anything
except the crack.
And the other ones,
the other cracks
might as well not be there,
buried under layer upon layer
of careful ice-cube coolness.

Woo woo — is he fooling you?
the original Mister Cool.
Did you ever see him
in his flat,
minus his this
            that
and the other?
Did you ever see him
when no one else is there?
In a mirror.
Did he look like you?
But not for long,
the ice-pack goes back on,
Mother of God,
You couldn't look like that,
I mean — you couldn't.

People would surely know,
the game is up,
people would surely go
straight to the heart

of the matter,
shatter shatter
suddenly you're deafened
by the clatter of broken ice
and that's not easy, casual
or nice but God almighty
it's a start.

Woo woo — I'm looking at you,
. . . and I love you.

NOBODY IS WHISTLING IN THE LABOUR EXCHANGE

Nobody is whistling in the Labour Exchange.

I'm avoiding eye contact with all the eyes
avoiding meeting mine.
No one is looking at anybody
yet everyone sees everybody else.

The entire building is securely anchored
to a pencil with a piece of string.
A lot of men are tied to the building
with something infinitely stronger.

I rattled a collection box at the girl
behind the counter. She put 10p in the box
and bought a flag. A lot of men cheered.
I think we'd won some sort of victory.
When we reached Hatch 8 we signed it away again.

HAPPY BIRTHDAY TO YOU

The after-midnight yahoos
echo around the Irish town,
the after-midnight yahoos
echo
when all the drinks gone down
and you drown and drown
and drown
because you haven't got
a woman.
Walking home though hedgerows
crooked as she goes
and God alone knows
what you'd do
if you had your way
with Brady's daughter
or anybody else.
But now it's after midnight
and your yahoos echo
all around the town
and into bedrooms
where you'll never go
and girls who sleep alone
are having fantasies
with their fingers.
It's better by yourself
than not at all
and when you fall asleep
you won't set eyes
upon a woman
until your mother
calls you in the morning
and wishes you Happy Birthday.
Today you are fifty eight.

AUTOMATIC CLICK CLICK

Early morning railway station.
An infinite number of Briefcase and Brollymen
(B & Bs) click through the turnstiles
NOW READ ON:

Automatic
Click click,
B & B
Click click,
B & B
Click click
. . . stuck!
Push, wriggle, pull.
Train coming,
B & B,
Well and truly
Panic-stricken
Stuck!
"Come on,
Shift yourself!
We've got appointments to keep,
     schedules to meet,
     things to do,
     with reference to,
And you're well and truly stuck!"
"Fix brollies!
Remember the 10th Ultimo!
Chaaaaaaarge!"

Human tide of B & Bs,
Cut, concuss, clamber,
Stampede, trample, pour,
All over stuck.
Onto the station,
Into the train,
And off towards
the eternal reward at 65.

Moments before
he expired,
stuck whispered two words.
". . . I . . . resign."

"Sure your job'll be gone
by now anyway,"
said the porter
who went into the hut
for a mug of tea and
a cheese sandwich.
"I'll phone the ambulance
after me break."

YOU SHOULDN'T HAVE TOLD ME

You called me into your flat.
"I'm going to commit suicide" you said.
"I'm off to the supermarket right now
to buy a bottle of Harpic."

"And I'm going into my flat
to write a poem. I hope you
don't do it. I'll miss you."

The supermarket was sold out of Harpic
so you got drunk instead.

I couldn't write a single word
so I'm going to hang myself.
But I'm not telling you about it.
You'll probably write a bloody poem.

MAD MEN DO IT OUT LOUD

Lusty lungs,
a lunatic alone,
raw red roaring
thunderthroat.
Happy as a hatter
and a million times as mad.
Damning Dublin,
bellowing at building sites,
fucking the begrudgers
and frighten-flapping
away the pigeons.

I can hear you shouting
but I won't let you know that.

Trying to tumble down
the towering crane
with the thunder of your threats.
Damning D-Day
the longest day
any day
a day like this day
is as mad as any other.
Now your curse the mother
that bore you,
with a final roar
you deafen Daniel O'Connell.
We can hear you
But we won't let you know that.
Raw red roaring
disturbs more than the peace.
We prefer to shout in silence.

FROGS

Frogs have been following me everywhere.
Black shiny frogs
peering out from under parked cars,
glistening, throats pulsing,
tongues flickering wet mucous
Christ — don't let them catch me.
Crowding on the pavement,
crushing together to leave me
only a narrow passage.
Fall to the left or the right
and we've got you.
You'll slip and slide for ever.
Bulging throats, bodies unclean.
Sandpaper yourself —
You won't get rid of us.
Tear off your skin,
we'll still be there.
We're watching you from
dark laneways.
We know you.

We'll leave you alone for a while now.
Peace.
We'll leave you peace for a while.
We're tired too.

THAT WAS HIS SECOND ONE

"I was wrong" he said.
"I made a mistake."
"You did, you did, you did, you did.
Kill him, kill him, kill him, kill him."

THE MAN IN THE NEXT BED

And I was saying out loud
"I wonder where David has gone."
And he was hiding his face
behind the curtain.
And it was shaking
with his laughter.
And when he showed his face
it was happy.
And then he hid it again.
Hiding and seeking with me.
And David is 23.

David sits in bed,
playing little laughing games
with his fingers.
Closely examining his hands.
Suddenly stopping
to stare at something
that nobody else can see
Smiling because it's beautiful
then suddenly clapping his hands
and hiding his face from me.
And David is 23.

He hunches over his jigsaw,
and finger-shuffles each piece.
Then fumbles it
and fondles it
and finds the fragment
pleases him
because the fragment fits.
Then suddenly he's staring
and clapping hands with glee.
It's time for hiding and seeking.
And David is 23.

He opens his mouth
for jerky sounds
and broken bits of speech.
He only knows one sentence.
He repeats and repeats and repeats.
"It wasn't me,
It wasn't me."
And David is 23.

YOU DON'T COME AROUND ANYMORE

The way you came to my flat
at half past six in the morning
because I was getting an early train
to Cork or somewhere.
"I brought you some sandwiches" you said.
Nobody ever loved me like that before.

You took away my pillowcase
and when you brought it back
you had washed and ironed it.
I wasn't used to people doing
things like that for me.
Nobody ever loved me like that before.

You don't come around anymore.
And I miss you.
I miss you more than I have ever missed anybody.

If you are making sandwiches
for somebody else
I hope they choke him.
I'm an awful bastard really.

BELFAST EARLY MORNING

Early morning soldier,
kneeling at the corner.
Maybe in a church
he would take off
his beret.
But he's not.
He's kneeling
at the corner
praying
with his rifle.
"Please God
if someone tries
to shoot me
grant me thy
Divine Assistance
to shoot him first."
I've seen his face before,
in Luton or was it Reading
or was it him at all?
His early morning mates
are searching cars.
They all look the same
on a cold grey
rifle clutching
car searching
white-knuckled
Belfast soldier
morning.
"An 18 year old soldier was today . . ."
God didn't hear his prayer.
Or maybe He did.
I don't know which side He's on.
He never really said.

NICE LIGHT SPRINKLY RAIN

"Yes" she said.
"I like it when it rains . . .
Not too heavy though . . .
Nice . . .nice light sprinkly rain."

God, he thought, will she never be
finished on that phone?"

"Makes the flowers grow . . .
and the carrots . . .
they need it like . . .
rain . . . to grow.
Not too heavy though . . .
nice and light and sprinkly."

You are holding the most
boring insignificant conversation
I have ever heard.
Will you for God's sake
get off that phone.

When she had finished
delivering her coded message
she did just that.

"Sorry for keeping you" she said.

Next morning
Fifty handpicked mercenaries
carried out 'Operation Nice
Light Sprinkly Rain'.
They took Government buildings,
The Central Post Office,
The International Airport and
The Agricultural Research Station
Where they put all the carrots to death.

Then it rained.
Nice light sprinkly rain.

I DECLARE TO GOD

Awake alive and high as a kite,
Don't think I'll sleep much tonight
    if at all.
God but it's late
    and everybody I know is asleep.
Suppose I could give somebody a ring
and get them out of bed
and say — "Hey — I know it's 4 o'clock
    and stuff like that.
4 o'clock and eh — how's it going?
   What's the story?
What?
No — I don't suppose it is so fucking funny.
    How's it going anyway?

Oh — I see.
  And also with you."
Suppose I could ring the Samaritans
   and say
"A friend of mine just said he'd wring my scraggy neck
so I've got a problem
    will you come round
    and we'll talk about it?
What?
Yeah . . . yeah . . . suppose I cut my wrists . . .
You'd come round then? Fair enough . . . and give me
 some soup?
No — listen — on second thoughts
    I'll call the talking clock.
And it'll tell me it's 4.30
    and it won't threaten
to wring my scraggy neck or anything.
Yeah — I think that's what I'll do.
Shit — no 10ps left.
        999 is free.
        I'll ring 999 and they'll say
"Which service please?"

                              So I'll have to set fire
                              to the bloody flat first . . .
                              Hell
                                      no matches.
Think I'll talk to God.
"Hello . . . God . . . what? . . . No — it's me . . . eh Pat . . .
eh . . . Pat Ingoldsby . . . P A T . . .
eh . . . I bought a black baby once . . .
Men's Sodality . . . 1959 . . .
What? You can't sleep either?
You want someone to talk to . . .
Yeah — that's O.K. . . . no trouble . . .
Flat One . . . ring the top bell.
"BBBBBBBBBBIIIIIIINNNNNGGGG!"
Jesus — that was quick.

                       REQUIEM

                 Legs like matchsticks
                 Snap! Snap!
                 They're broken.

                 Long bony fingers
                 In litter-bins pokin'.

                 Sleeps under cardboard
                 by rats awoken.

                 Knocks back cheap wine
                 on vomit she's chokin'.

                 When they found her
                 a sort of prayer was spoken.

                 . . . "Jaysus!"

                         99

DEATH OF A LIBERATOR

He went into the fishmonger's shop
where they sold 'Live Crabs'.
They were on a tray,
limbs feebly moving.
When the woman's back was
turned he whispered it.
"Right lads — now's your chance."
They scampered down Vernon Avenue
between lines of cheering people.
A woman sang "Onward Christian Soldiers'.
One by one they careered down the
sailing club ramp.
The commodore cheered and fired his cannon.
It decapitated the man who
had led the crabs to freedom.
"Feck it anyway," said the woman
in the fish shop. "Now I'll never
get paid."

THIRTY SEVEN YEARS

He had never lost his temper,
never, never, never,
for thirty seven years.
They sat on him,
spat on him,
deriled and defiled
and called him fool.
Do this that and the other,
fool.
Now do the other, that and this,
now that this and the other,
Now start again.
He had never lost his temper
for thirty seven years.
Which made it all the more terrible
when he did.
Nobody who heard it will ever forget
the roar.
"EEEEEEEEEEEEAAAAAAAAAAAAAAAA"
When it faded away,
three men lay
dead.
The broken-boned clasped their
broken bones.
He opened his mouth to roar again,
but this time it was
a whisper.

WITHOUT YOUR CROSS YOU COULD
BE ANYONE

An unruly looking beggar
stood beside a nun
in the bus queue.
Long hair, tangled beard
but no cross on his back.
She moved away.
He shouldn't have left
his cross at home.
she might have called him
"Master"
and given him the price
of a cup of tea.
Without your cross
you could be anybody.
You probably are.

A QUESTION OF INNOCENCE

"Everybody's looking at me,
I think I'm going mad,"
He thought about a place to hide,
And remembered a place he'd had,
safe and warm and far from fear,
safe and warm and secure,
"I think I'll visit Mammy,
She'll know the place, that's for sure."

Mammy was opening a tin of beans,
when into the kitchen he slid
looking for his safe and sound,
seeking the place he had hid.

He knew it was round here somewhere,
on the sofa or up in his room,
Mammy said "Yes son — that's the place,
Or Bandon, or Gort or Khartoom!"

"There's something you're not telling me,"
He said it both easy and slow,
"I've tried looking under a cabbage,
There's something that I need to know."

Mammy felt faintly uneasy,
and tightened her grip on her broom,
There's nothing as lonesome or fearsome or sad,
As Junior's return to the womb.

She watched him walk into the night,
She watched him and later she cried,
"What with himself and all of his brothers as well,
There'd be standing room only inside!"

GOOD THIEF HANGING HIGH

I met a lot of goodness
behind the high wall
in Mountjoy Jail.
And I went in
and I was able
to come out again.
All the lads went
down to bed
and I was going home.
Feeling very very sad
and very much alone.
I met the sort of honesty
that cuts you to the bone.
And if you've never fallen
and if you've never known
an agony in your garden
you have little business going
behind the wall in Mountjoy Jail.
Where the the good thief's hanging high,
a six-inch nail in either hand
and a wild laugh in his eye.

LOCKED IN

Morning without pity
finds the yawning night nurse,
wraith-like white nurse,
flitting through the sometime waking,
restless sleeping, bed-spring-creaking
world of broken minds.

Morning without mercy
finds separated from his wife,
severed wrists with desperate knife,
quietly cursing pints too many,
future without any
hope of ever calling
house a home.

Morning without peace
finds the sobbing strong man,
left alone too long,
stumbling through a nightmare world
of fright where fearful phantoms
mock his tangled thought.

Morning passes slowly,
for the proud and for the lowly,
vacant staring, some past caring,
minute counting, tension mounting,
corridor pacing, tranquility chasing,
when will it be night?
Today they won't let us go home,
but perhaps tomorrow they might,
today they won't let us go home,
but perhaps tomorrow they might.

YOU HAVE TO LAUGH OR NOT

Some people laugh when nothing is funny
and they really want to cry.
Some people laugh when they think that
you think they should be laughing even
though they haven't a clue what the joke is.
Some people think that something is very funny
but they stop themselves from laughing
because nobody else is.
I think this is one of the saddest pieces
I have ever written and I nearly died laughing
while I was writing it.
If I was a court jester they'd chop my head off.

2 a.m. CORK STATION

There was nobody coming or going
as he crooked shuffled
onto Cork Railway Station.
The trains had stopped hours ago.
All the people who don't crooked
shuffle around Cork City were
home in their beds.
But he didn't sleep.
He sat on a bench
and told his raggy story
to the echoes and the moths
around the lights.
You couldn't see his head
for hair and beard and
dirty brown duffle coat.
I don't think he wanted
a million pounds.
I think he wanted someone
to listen.

So I stood beside him.
And he looked up.
And he spoke to me.
"Fuck off" he said.

I WANT TO SEE A WHALE

I met a man on a bus
who sees big things
inside his head.
"Whenever I get elated"
he said.
"I see huge whales.
And wires —

Long electric wires
that connect me up
To Russia and China
and places like that."

The only time I ever see
things inside my head
is when I feel depressed.
And then I only see
Emaciated sardines.

I would love to see
a huge whale. It'd be a sure sign that
my depression is clearing up.

God — I'd love to see a huge
whale inside my head. A
medium sized one would do.
But I won't tell my doctor that.
He'd surely change my medication.

PROPOSITION TO A SPIDER

Spider — little black spider,
No one is as lonesome as you,
Every time I see you,
You're all on your own,
I can't imagine what you're going to do.

You appear up there in the corner,
And walk upside down on my roof,
But you only ever do it by yourself,
Are you shy and insecure or just aloof?

Why do you never wander in pairs,
Do you all hate each other or what?
I don't expect you to hold each other's hand,
But we all need all the friends that we've got.

I feel very sad when I watch you,
Tiny, oh so tiny, and alone,
Maybe that's the way you spiders like it,
Maybe you feel better on your own.

I've just had a very good idea,
It's sort of about me and you,
If you'll be my special eight-legged friend,
I'll be your special friend too.

WITH APOLOGIES TO THE ANIMALS

In the zoo
we watched a bee
landing on a flower
beside a butterfly.
The flower bending
with the weight
of the bee.
In the zoo
we watched a baby
studying its shadow
on the grass until
the sun went in
behind a cloud.
In the zoo
we watched a spider
checking its web
for captive flies
and finding only
raindrops.
One of these days
I'll get around to the animals
but it will have to be
with somebody else.

THE ULTIMATE SELF-PITY POEM

Everyone else is better than me and I'm no good
at anything. There's no point in trying because
I'll only fail.
MOAN.
I'm not going to talk to anyone because I
can't think of anything to say. Besides, other
people's silences are much more articulate
than mine.
MOAN AND SIGH.
I'm completely finished and it's all downhill
from now on. My hill on which it's all down
isn't nearly as steep as other people's.
MOAN SIGH AND MOAN AGAIN.
Other people are spectacular failures. I'm
only a very ordinary one. I wallow in self-
pity. Other people drown magnificently in
theirs.
SOB AND TREMBLE.
My psychiatrist doesn't understand the grave
nature of my disturbances. He goes away for
five weeks holidays and doesn't give me the
number of his hotel.
LOOK TRAGIC.
If anyone else wrote this poem, everybody
would say — "Isn't it great." But because I
wrote it, they're saying — "He even makes a
balls out of being negative."
COLLAPSE.

This is the other end of the book.
The other end is at the other end.